To my family
I am sorry

Sarah Smith

# My Name Is Sarah
# I am an Alcoholic

AUSTIN MACAULEY
PUBLISHERS LTD.

A CIP catalogue record for this title is available from the British Library.

ISBN 978 1 78455 362 3 (Paperback)
ISBN 978 1 78455 364 7 (Hardback)

www.austinmacauley.com

First Published (2015)
Austin Macauley Publishers Ltd.
25 Canada Square
Canary Wharf
London
E14 5LB

Printed and bound in Great Britain

# Author's Note

As in any story there has to be an end and you have to say to yourself enough is enough and that you have it given it your best shot.

I have written this book to help people try and understand what addiction is and also for alcoholics that good can come out of bad.

We all come in different sizes and shapes and cultures, we look no different to you while sober.

When you see a homeless person, a tramp or a drunk, please think that they may be the unlucky ones and this disease has taken their mind and soul, ravished their very being.

I am one of the lucky ones and came out of this madness. This is my story. I give it to you.

Thank you.

# Addendum

I am not ashamed to be an alcoholic; I am ashamed of what I did through the influence of alcohol.

After all the trauma in my life I eventually realised what my spare hand was for.

To write and illustrate children's books, to paint and to draw.

This made me feel complete. It was instrumental in my recovery, the diversion I needed.

I have also designed bookmarks, soft toys and wallpaper to accompany my books.

I am confident in my artistic ability, but I sometimes wonder where my inspiration came from, I find it hard to believe it was I, but it was.

It feels good to be positive, and that can't be bad.

If I stop smoking I would have another free hand and who knows what I may be able to achieve?

There comes a time when writing you have to say enough is enough and that you have given your best shot, and I have.

This is my story and I give it to you.

# Synopsis

My name is Sarah, I am an alcoholic.
On entering Alcoholics Anonymous I felt I had been branded with the word alcoholic on my forehead, stamped there for everyone to see.
But, I was a person behind the word alcoholic.
I felt like a piece of cattle on the way to be slaughtered.
Unfortunately that was exactly what I was doing to myself.
I was living a very painful and slow death, with everyone who loved me watching me slowly killing myself.
I can divide alcoholism into three stages.
The first stage being taking that first drink and getting drunk, drinking more than others but unaware you are doing so.
Then escalating into the second stage.
I am now dependent on alcohol, this is a gradual decline.
I am now entering the third stage of alcoholism.
This is the part where you can't stop shaking, you feel so ill you think you are dying.
Your whole body screaming for alcohol and death.
Your mind and body are so exhausted you have no fight left.
I was lucky, my family ferociously fought for my life, which meant something to them.
It meant nothing to me anymore.
You can be affected by what is called a wet brain, you drool, you are incapable of moving. Soiling yourself where you lay.
You can begin to hallucinate, seeing pink elephants as it was once called.
I was at risk of losing my children, my parents, my twin sister and home.
I didn't care, I just wanted to die.

# My mam

She died in Dad's arms just as it should be.
I will remember my mam when the sun rises and sets.
I will remember my mam when the breeze rustles the leaves and crunch under foot.
I will remember my mam when I hear a giggle or a laugh.
My mam lives on in my heart and soul.
At night she sleeps with angels and watches over me.
I will love my mam until my dying day, where she waits for me with arms outstretched just as it should be.
Here we are one year on and I miss you just as much.
Here we are one year on and my heart aches just as much.
Here we are one year on since we held you close as you said your last goodbye.
Here we are one year on and the leaves are falling all around me in an autumnal cascade, leaves crunching underfoot.
Here we are one year on and the changing colours of autumn remind me of you keeping me safe giving me solace knowing you are all around me, loving me.
Here we are one year on and I know I will see you again,
Save a place for me.


# Hello Mam

Here we are in your final resting place.
You can hear the children playing in the park and birds singing overhead.
You are with me in my heart and soul and I know you are near me when everyday life's little coincidences remind me of you and I say,
"Hello Mam," and smile.
Here we are another year gone
I have your wedding photo in my living room.
I look at you and Dad each day.
You are both smiling,
So I smile
I wear your wedding ring with pride.
It links you with Dad and me to both of you.
Sleep tight Mam with my everlasting love.

# Chapter One

My name is Sarah and I am an alcoholic. I have been sober for over seventeen years.

As in any other illness, it can be considered a journey. I don't like that word; to me it signifies a jaunt, an expedition which alcoholism is not.

To me it reaches the depths of depravity a dependency into a void, a black hole with no way out, no escapes, and no prospects.

It grips you round the throat, strangling the life out of you.

How I have stayed sober for this long is an enigma.

My first daughter went to live with her father aged 14. I dealt with this by my brain shutting this out.

It had broken my heart, my second daughter went to live with her father aged 16, and my brain also shut this out.

It had broken my heart. My brain seemed to do this involuntarily. My son and I were all that was left of our family.

My mother died just over a year ago and without this lady I would have lost everything.

My grief was uncontrollable. It is amazing what the brain is capable of, shutting pain out, which probably saved my life.

Throughout all this I didn't drink.

It doesn't mean it has been easy; to the contrary, it has been unyielding.

Society is left with an immense drinking problem, yet it is still advertised.

Smoking is not advertised anymore, why not drink?!

It ruins so many lives, not just the alcoholics, but families and friends as well.

Drinking games are advertised on the Internet, actively encouraging youngsters to drink, often being fatal.

I have witnessed my children playing these games.

All of my children drink a lot, it is said alcoholism is hereditary, have I passed this on to my children? I have to live with this thought every day of my life.

Yet, it can also be a learned behaviour, my ex-husband's family drinks heavily, visibly displaying alcohol.

I stopped drinking when my children were five, seven and nine.

I like to think they were too young to remember my intoxication, unfortunately they do.

My alcoholism became the excuse for everything and I had walked straight into a trap of my own doing.

Their father told my children that this was the cause of the breakdown of our marriage.

Nothing can be further from the truth.

I didn't start drinking again until after the divorce.

If I feel like a drink now, I have to think in a split second how ill I was, and so close to death's door, its ugly hand stretching towards me, enticing me back.

# Chapter Two

I was born on the 1/4/1956, one hour after my twin sister; I popped out and said "April fool".

I weighed 3lb 2oz and my twin at 4lb 3oz. We were adopted at five months old.

My father had asked for a day off work, when asked why he said it was to bring his "twin daughters home".

As my dad didn't own a car at this time his boss said he could use his car and driver to bring us home.

We had arrived in style. Both of us must have been little fighters as there was no premature delivery equipment, like there is today.

We had always known we had been adopted, the adoption agency had advised us of this.

My parents told us we had been chosen and that we were special.

I had never questioned that we may have siblings until my sister mentioned this.

I didn't even question that we had another dad.

Regarding my biological mother, my supposition was that she was too young and due to moral principles in the fifties the stigma would be great.

My parents have faults like everyone else, but I love them and am proud they are my parents.

I often wonder what may have happened to us if our parents hadn't chosen us because I certainly gave them a roller coaster ride that they wouldn't forget in a hurry.

I remember my dad telling me in one adoption interview he asked, "What is the prospect of adopting twins?" and twins he got.

Apparently there is a high risk of alcoholism in adopted twins: Having said that my twin hasn't inherited this disease, alcoholism.

I was very ill as a child with bronchitis and suffered terribly with childhood illnesses.

I remember to this day being covered from head to foot with chicken pox, and was incensed that my twin had the same time off school as me, she had seven spots.

We also had mumps and measles, which you are inoculated against today.

The doctor said I would outgrow bronchitis. Which I did, only to be replaced by tonsillitis, and so many colds; I think I had every strain going which went hand in hand with cold sores.

When all of this subsided I suffered with hay fever for several years, eventually that went as well.

Health wise I was no further forward.

Obviously I had a lot of time off school and missed out in the basics of maths and English, which I believe is why I have no concept of maths today. I like to think I caught up with English as I gained an O level in English language and English literature.

In our maths class everyone had to stand up and if you gave the correct answer you could sit down. I always stayed upright, the last one standing, which didn't help my confidence.

I remember my dad trying to teach me maths for my O level; I always ended up in tears and my dad scratching his head in disbelief.

Suffice to say I failed everything apart from art.

I was so distressed over exams my mam took me to see the doctor who prescribed medication and this was the beginning of my dependency on prescribed medicated drugs.

I also remember asking the doctor about an operation on my nose. He said my nose was perfectly all right.

# Chapter Three

It was a long time before the "we" became "I".

Because I was a sickly child I got more attention.

It is no fun being ill and I spent many a birthday in bed.

I remember to this day the taste of that medicine; unfortunately it used to make me sick, which prolonged my illness.

As I was ill so much I became quite introverted, very much self-absorbed.

I spent a lot of time inside looking out, whilst I was lying there suffering.

In twins there is usually one stronger than the other and that job fell to my twin.

I had no identity, no confidence, but I didn't have to, my sister had enough for the both of us.

I was like a puppet with everyone else pulling the strings, but I knew no different.

My twin made all of our decisions and I followed her around like a lost puppy. I wonder how she felt about this. But like me, she knew no different.

My sister would organize everything for me, even my school satchel.

Her friends were my friends.

This was just natural to me and I didn't question this, I just accepted it.

I, of course, would rather be my twin; she is more assertive, kinder and prettier than me.

We are fraternal twins and look totally different from our head down to our toes; we don't even look like sisters.

Our tastes and styles differ, if she liked white, I liked black.

I had no idea how to stand on my own two feet. I still ask questions today instead of thinking it through.

When I tell people I am a twin, they say "oh no, not another one".

My dad still refers to me as his "wayward daughter".

The next part of this book I have called "twinisms", perhaps I have coined a new word.

These are my memories of incidents when we were growing up.

Once we were sent to bed early, we had been playing dressing up with mam's clothes.

Obviously they were too big for us and we argued over a safety pin.

In those days we were told, "wait until your father gets home", but he was as soft as Mam.

I remember cutting my sisters hair and hiding behind the settee.

I decided once we had decided to have separate bedrooms, I burst a hot water bottle so I could go back with my twin.

I even remember what I used, it was Easter and it was a little stick with a chicken for a head.

I always seemed to have to sit on the plug end of the bath, so I packed a little case, putting my teddy bear in and marched up the road, my mother following behind me.

I still have my teddy, she is a bit threadbare as she is 58 years old, and I called her Tessa, my sister called hers Bruno.

For some reason I can remember my clothes.

We had some beautiful ones, a sundress which was blue and white, another having Scotty dogs around the hem.

I love blue and white, and Scotty dogs today.

Also we had a twin pram and my mam used to take us to see the pigs on a farm, I was too young to remember this but I love pigs.

My mam used to make a lot of clothes and knit us jumpers.

I think it was a race to see whose she would finish first.

My mam used to work for a tailor and everything she did she worked to a very high standard.

At Easter time we would paint paste eggs to roll down a suitable hill, I remember once I had bronchitis and couldn't join in.

At that point of time if you suffered with this ailment you didn't exercise and my mam wrote several notes to the P.E teacher excusing me from joining in.

I didn't like gymnastics and I used my notes to prolong this.

Having said that I enjoyed netball and other outside sports.

My sister enjoyed sports and became a P.E teacher.

I also remember being given the bumps on our birthday. It was so embarrassing, your blouse buttons would open, and your skirt went up to your chin showing your knickers.

I have never enjoyed my birthday until after 12 o'clock midday; you are only an April fool before midday so I couldn't get out of that one.

Jokes would be played upon us, wrapped parcels with nothing inside. We didn't always have to share a present; I only remember this happening once when we were given a musical jewellery case with a ballerina in a tutu.

After 12 o'clock, I relaxed.

Apparently I suffered from 'stop breaths', I would hold my breath until I fainted.

My mam took me to Great Ormand Street children's hospital for tests, in which electrodes were placed around my head.

Nothing was wrong and it was deemed to be tantrums.
My twin was knock-kneed, but we won't go there.

# Chapter Four

We had moved to Welwyn Garden City, near London, when we were two years old.

I don't remember much, but what I do remember is when we had started school, I asked the maths teacher a question and rubbed my chin.

He asked if I was growing a beard.

I was so sensitive with remarks like this I probably thought I was growing one.

When it was our birthday we had to go on stage to receive a birthday card, I remember they had bunnies on them.

Of course I was beside myself with embarrassment, I blushed readily and couldn't find where I was sitting, I was mortified.

We moved to Nottingham aged eleven, the eleven plus had been abolished, so luckily I had avoided that as I am sure I would have failed.

We attended a school in Ruddington. One of my worst memories of this was that there was a new ruling that twins should be separated.

I was frogmarched to the 'B' class.

This had a profound effect on me, but I did well and had to be returned to the 'A' class.

One good thing to come from this school is that we had to learn to write in italics and my handwriting improved considerably, I became proud of this and can still write in italics today.

We then moved to a comprehensive school called Rushcliffe. I remember the English teacher had a lovely Welsh accent.

He had asked my sister and I if we would babysit.

We said yes and on our return as I was shutting the gate, he told me he liked me a lot and would like to see me again.

I ran into the house as fast as I could.

I used to have a Saturday job in a green grocer. Whilst I was in the back of the shop the owner put his hand up my blouse and said, "You are skinny aren't you?"

I ran out of the shop as fast as I could, another assistant caught up with me and asked me to return and she would make sure I was never on my own.

I had no life skills to deal with these incidents.

I never told my parents and eventually I left and worked in a shoe shop and was met with all kinds of foot horrors.

I was the type of person who always wanted to be someone else; I was never satisfied being me.

I wanted longer blonder hair, I wanted to be less skinny and I wanted my sister's nose.

Years later I realised that I was exactly who I wanted to be.

A school friend described me as being stunning, but that didn't matter, any compliments washed over me. I didn't feel like that person and no amount of compliments changed my attitude,

At school I was called Pinocchio, I was told I had a high forehead and that I was so skinny I was lucky that my legs didn't snap.

So, I was the nose with a high forehead on sticks and to add to this mixture, with spots.

I had heard all the skinny jokes you could think of.

Why do people make us feel like that?

But, I supposed it was my nature. Children can be very cruel and to some, these comments would be ignored.

I was well into my twenties before I showed my legs.

At the age of fifteen knee boots and maxi dresses were in fashion, and these suited me.

I remember a photograph was taken with me next to a donkey, and we had the same legs, which I joked about when I was older.

I found out that my sister had kept this photograph, I had been right, the donkey and I had the same legs.

# Chapter Five

I found it very difficult going through puberty.

I became depressed and uncertain about life. There was a girl at school who used to play my twin and I against each other. I was always called Pinocchio and that I had a high forehead and I was so skinny I was lucky my legs didn't break. So I was this nose with a high forehead on sticks.

I also thought that I didn't have many boyfriends. On reading an old diary I had at least nine over a year.

It is very sad I thought so little about myself.

They say you never forget your first love, which was true for me.

It was an on-off relationship; it was always back on if I found another boyfriend.

We used to pass love letters to each other via his sister, I still have these letters today and I have kept all my own diaries.

He wrote a poem for me:

Maggie was not tall

But all the same she wasn't small

As she detested school as much as her name

Twig she was called

Everyone knows her simply as 'Twig'

Small but not tall

But very thin

Very thin indeed

Maggie hated life,

To breathe, to see or touch

Anyone of anything

Especially boys, smirking grinning four eyed faces

Knocked out teeth

With black holes gaping

But deep down in others, the minds of thinkers

Twig would eventually blossom and show a bright array of colour.

He had won an award for this but it must be said, I had all my teeth!

One time when our relationship was on an off stage, I took an overdose of tablets my doctor had prescribed.

I remember my sister saying she couldn't wake me up, but I did wake up and I was only a bit groggy and no harm done.

I am totally ashamed of this incident, but it had happened and I had to deal with it.

With my first love came my first sexual experience, all I remember is that it felt weird?

I also got Cystitis, which is known as the 'honeymoon ailment', just my luck?

I think this is around the time alcohol came knocking on my door and stayed.

My parents had been out at the time, I can't remember why I had a drink, but I had.

I remember being sick on the carpet in my bedroom. When my parents returned I said I had felt sick, but couldn't be, so I had had a drink.

This was the beginning of lying. Was I believed? I don't know.

I drank until I was sick then drank again and was sick again. This drinking bout rendered me comatose on the settee for two days. It also made me remember, this was the time I was also taking medication for depression.

This would be a lethal concoction that later in my life would have devastating consequences.

For some strange reason I remember my dad saying that if you had had too much to drink and you were dizzy to stare at one spot in the room.

As alcohol embedded itself into my psyche, the dizziness ceased, along with my brain.

# Chapter Six

As I had failed all my exams apart from art, I applied for a course in art, whereby I would study art for half of the week, the other half I studied three O levels and four A levels.

There was a lecturer from the school I had attended in Ruddington, and he gave me a chance.

I enrolled on the course and can honestly say that the next two years were the best years of my life.

This was the first time I had been separated from my twin.

I developed a personality of my own and grew into a young woman.

There were about fifteen of us on this course and we became a unit.

For the first year we all studied art in general, the second year we had to choose a specialised subject and I chose graphic design. I learned silkscreen printing, etching, in fact all sorts of mediums and I received a grade A in my A level.

I developed my drawing skills and an imagination I hadn't thought I could be capable of.

Stick me in an art room cupboard and I am in my element.

I remember our group had to draw a nude model, not one of us had drawn the nipples.

We also had to draw a nude male, but he kept his boxers on.

As I was taking three O levels and four A levels I was advised to drop one O level in physics and an A level in sociology.

I wish I hadn't been advised to do this, but I was seventeen and just followed the advice.

It was a shame because I really enjoyed sociology, but the decision had been made.

I passed English language and English literature at O level and graphic design, art and art history, which I also enjoyed.

I was nervous taking these exams and in oral English the teacher helped me by choosing a picture I liked, 'Starry Night' by Vincent Van Gogh.

I cried throughout the whole episode, mumbling my way through.

Hopefully I got a mark for remembering my name?

Luckily this was only part of the exam and I passed.

I had studied *Animal Farm* by George Orwell, *The Merchant of Venice* by Shakespeare and a book called *The Horse's Mouth* by an artist.

Our art group used to attend parties together and outings to the pub, we all got 'tipsy'.

Even though we were under age we were always served alcohol, restrictions weren't as important, unlike today.

At one party my boyfriend decided to throw me down the stairs. He eventually passed out, sucking his thumb, so that was the end of that relationship.

He was seventeen years old.

Another boy at that party started talking to me; I remember him and others sitting on the floor rolling joints using a record sleeve.

I had no interest in drugs as they frightened me, it is very sad I became addicted to one of the worst drugs around, alcohol.

I started dating this boy for the next three years and as he worked he had enough money to buy drinks for both of us.

I learnt later on in our relationship after he had taken me home, he would meet like-minded people to smoke cannabis.

I became engaged to him and we started looking for a house together.

Deep down I realised I didn't want to get married to him.

After a lot of soul searching, I finished the relationship.

He was so distraught at this and by then I could drive, he followed me everywhere, holding a sign up to his car window saying that he loved me.

Throughout the ensuing years I believe he became an alcoholic.

I hope he combated this otherwise he could be dead, or so wracked with this wretched disease and the problems that alcohol brings.

There is no way out with this illness and it brings with it the surmountable complications that ravage our bodies.

# Chapter Seven

After leaving college at eighteen I had applied to study Graphic Design at an art college.

At this point our group hadn't taken any exams, and at one interview I was told I was taking too much on.

I was upset by this and felt I hadn't been given a chance.

Students could apply to enter what was called a 'pool' and if any placements became available you would be considered.

My sister had applied for teachers training and was accepted.

My dad started out as a lecturer, and me being I, I just followed.

This was a bad decision on my part and I know my life would have been so different if I had just waited for a place at a school.

Patience had never been my strong point.

So, off I went to study at a teachers training college at Walsall, near Birmingham.

It was the first college in the country whereby you could attain a degree in two years by studying 'modules'.

I always achieved an A in art, and usually a C in other modules, which was adequate.

I over drank at college, but so did a lot of students.

It wasn't ruining my life at this point and I had no idea how my life would spiral out of control in the years to come.

There was a lot of time in my life where I felt I didn't fit in, and teachers training college was no different.

This of course was due to my insecurities, my anxieties and that no one would like me.

Whilst in teacher training I had left my boyfriend in Nottingham, he would visit every weekend and after a year I transferred to a college nearer home.

After the first term I knew teaching wasn't for me.

At a school placement I had to read a story to young children without a book in front of me.

I remember being told one child was obsessed with water. He had asked me if he could go to the toilet. I said yes and off he went to turn on all of the taps.

Then another child had also asked to go to the toilet, all the children's hands went up to use the bathroom.

I had lost control of the class.

I wasn't just nervous, I had been terrified. I was appalled at myself.

I can really laugh about this now and how a bunch of five year olds could reduce me to tears?

Everything went down the toilet after that.

We had to write about inflation and deflation, I put myself under so much stress, I couldn't remember what was what?

I had got myself into such a pickle, I never returned to college again.

I was now unemployed, I was always striving to make my dad proud of me and I had let him down.

I would strive to do this the rest of my life and I feel I have never made him proud of me.

I would let him down over and over again.

It wasn't long before I secured a job in the civil service.

I enjoyed this job and quickly rose to the next level; I was now a clerical officer.

I made a lot of good friends but sometimes I couldn't shake the feeling of not belonging.

# Chapter Eight

I think I have always had someone to hide behind, certainly my parents and my twin sister.

I did the same with drink.

My family created a safety net and always cleaned up after me.

When I was twenty-four I met the love of my life, I adored him. I remember my mam saying that he could be hurt and to be careful, only the tables turned and it was me who was deeply wounded.

I always took a bottle of wine around to his home.

I think he may have had a glass, and then I drank the rest.

He wasn't a drinker, he played football, but I still drank. But for two years our relationship was marvellous and even though I still drank, I wasn't always blotto.

We had a holiday in Avon, and I know this was the time I became pregnant.

I read in a magazine that if you stop taking the pill it would be a couple of months before you could get pregnant as your body had to adjust so I thought no more about it.

When I told my boyfriend he said, "I suppose I will have to marry you then".

I knew he would only marry me because of the baby and not because he loved me.

I told my parents and I remember my mam telling me dad "eee Alan, she's pregnant".

My parents took over and it was decided that I would have an abortion and true to form the decision was made for me.

Was this the right decision? I don't know, but I was glad it was out of my hands.

Would my life have been different if I had married and had the baby, I don't know, but I like to think so?

One thing I do know is that I started drinking heavier.

We had a holiday in Corfu and I remember falling into some bushes and I stayed there a while, as you do.

I began to get drunk every time I had alcohol.

I guess this was my reaction to having an abortion.

My boyfriend had a decision to make, did he move to play professional football, or stay in his current employment.

For me there was only one answer, he had to give football a go.

I travelled every weekend, but this was not to last. In my heart I knew he had found someone else.

I was devastated and on our last night together, I tried to cut my wrist.

His words to me were, "whatever love I had for you before has gone".

So that was the end of that.

I was now in the grip of alcoholism.

My mother slept with me for a while, I was so distraught I kept waking up crying.

I was ill equipped to deal with the loss of a child, and to lose the father had been too much to bear.

I loved this many and still do today, twenty-five years later.

Eventually I moved on, only to receive a call from him asking me to go to a concert, I said no and that I had another boyfriend.

Would things have been different if I had said yes? I don't know.

So I had chosen the new boyfriend and drink.

Once again, heavy drinkers surrounded me.

I stayed with the next boyfriend for about two years.

He saw another girl about twice a week, he insisted this was a platonic relationship and in my naivety I believed him.

I had just moved into a new home and a friend of mine asked if she could use my home for a tryst. I agreed and gave her a key.

I later learnt it was my boyfriend she took to my home.

This was a married woman with two children.

One night when I was out drinking I saw them together and fuelled by drink I broke a glass and threatened them and told her husband to ask her why she had a key to my home.

Once again my dad had come and collected me and was told by this boyfriend, "your daughter drinks too much", which I did, but he drank excessively.

My boyfriend then went to hospital for a routine operation.

I went to visit him and sitting on his bed was his other girlfriend.

I was deeply hurt and finished the relationship; he asked me to stay and said he wouldn't see his other girlfriend.

I walked away straight into an abomination that would become my life.

I was by this time entering into the second stage of alcoholism and fuelled with tranquillizers had dangerous consequences.

In fact, I probably drank less than anybody else, but the combination had undesirable effects.

But, I am still an alcoholic and always will be.

After a while I met my husband to be, like me he was a heavy drinker.

We had mutual friends who also drank heavily.
So the cycle began again.

# Chapter Nine

Eventually my next boyfriend asked me to marry him. I said yes.

My parents advised against this and this fatal decision altered my life forever, nothing would ever be the same again.

My husband lost his job in Nottingham and his family encouraged him back to Sheffield, his hometown.

My alcoholism had been well known at my job in the civil service and I was treated well.

This meant it was harder for me to get a transfer.

Eventually I did but the executives and clerical officers spurned me.

I had doors shut in my face, every time I got out of my seat I was asked where I was going.

I used to give a lift to a girl I worked with. She was showing some photographs around.

I asked if I could have a look, she told me I didn't know anybody, turned around and ignored me.

I began to hate this job and didn't know why I was being treated like this.

My confidence plummeted, especially as one colleague followed me around the office, she obviously had nothing better to do, was she being followed as well?

She once reported me for drinking a coffee outside my lunchtime. We were able to drink when we wanted to.

I used to ring my mam when I arrived to work to let her know I was all right, this girl asked, "why do you ring your mam every day, is it in case you top yourself?" This was such a strange comment.

I later learned she had a nervous breakdown, but this girls sleuthing days were over.

I was a very passive person who wouldn't say boo to a goose, an easy target for bullies.

I did make one friend at lunchtime, we used to go to the pub together and guess what? I had a drink again and again and one for the road.

# Chapter Ten

I was at rock bottom.

I was so ill but I didn't know what was wrong with me.

I made an appointment with my doctor and told him of my concerns; he told me I was an alcoholic.

I didn't like what he said but at last I had a name for this illness.

I now became Margaret the alcoholic, Margaret the person had now gone.

You tend to home in upon like-minded people.

It was like having built an antenna.

It is said that you are an alcoholic the first time you drink.

Looking back I can't even imagine drinking that amount of fluid.

Drink slides up upon you, and, before you know what is happening, it gets you right where it hurts.

I know realise it was like I didn't have a stopcock; my brain wouldn't switch off and tell me I had had enough alcohol.

So, I carried on drinking.

At this time I likened my alcohol to drinking a bucket full of beer, whisky and brandy, in fact anything I could get my hands on.

The next day I would be so dehydrated I drank at least three pints of milk and orange juice. For some reason it had to be cold.

Once I accidently drank a bottle of turpentine, which was in a similar carton to the milk. Suffice to say I was sick; it was so greasy it was revolting.

I rang the doctor who had no idea what to advise me. He rang the poison unit who said as long as I had been sick I would be all right.

Drinking at this stage was ruining my life, snatching me in its claws with a grip so hard and tight you could not release yourself.

The doctor had given me a blood test to check my liver. Luckily the results were fine.

But, none of that mattered. Continuous use of alcohol causes cirrhosis of the liver and a whole lot of other problems, even cancer.

It can damage your brain, your eyes, in fact anything from your head down to your toes, whereby you can suffer gout and amputation.

The doctor gave me two weeks off work to help me recover.

I was also prescribed a drug called Antabuse, which, if mixed with alcohol, can result dire consequences.

Luckily I was frightened of what may happen, but only I could make this decision, and like any addict you would rather drink and kill yourself.

My brain was full of receptors going manic wanting alcohol.

I remember going to see my mam and telling her I was an alcoholic, she replied by asking what the real problem was and in a way she was right.

I had been affected by trauma in my life and found solace in alcohol, which momentarily numbed the pain.

It is hard to define, but, as an example, if you find a dress or a pair of shoes and you have to have them, you can't settle until you buy them, even if you cannot afford the resulting debt.

At this time, I was referred for counselling and had to report to a doctor once a week.

One such therapist didn't speak to me, it was up to me to talk and for her to listen; that didn't help, and I wanted feedback.

The doctor asked if I had had a drink, I said no and that was the end of that.

# Chapter Eleven

Whilst I was pregnant with my first child, I relapsed just the once.

The office in Nottingham was having a Christmas party and not being the one to miss out on the fun I drove down to Nottingham drunk with my best friend sitting in the passenger seat: A bottle of vodka.

As I neared Nottingham I clipped a car, I put my foot down and off I went.

Luckily, if this is the right word, I got away with it and no one was hurt.

I was proud to show off my bump and I loved being pregnant.

It was all I ever wanted - a husband, a home and a family.

This was nearly very cruelly taken away from me, and it wasn't through a drink.

Eventually I was in my usual state and a friend had rung my father and on his arrival I was unceremoniously removed from the office.

One friend said he would look after me, but my dad won.

At my parents' home I needed more alcohol, I ranted and raved and eventually, to my parents' relief, I fell asleep.

In the morning with my familiar hangover a flood of thoughts invaded my mind:

The guilt

The self-loathing

The disgust

The revulsion

The disgrace and the abomination that had become my life, it was an existence, an animation without me playing a part.

But here I was back again in the same pathetic excuse of a life.

I was a drunk

A lush

A boozer

A toper

A soak

A wino

A dipsomaniac,

And this is nothing to be proud of.

I felt unlovable; I developed a self-loathing and a hatred for myself that went so deep it crippled me.

Funnily enough if you look up the word drunk it offers such words as:

Tired

Emotional

Maudlin

Overemotional

Tearful and sentimental, and describes many more.

Yet to me a word I would like to describe myself is "a poor lost soul in a disease-ridden mind and body".

When I returned home to Sheffield I was full of regret. My husband forgave me, but he still continued to drink heavily.

I was on the phone that day ringing doctors, help groups, health centres; trying to find out if I had harmed my baby.

As I was in the second trimester, I wouldn't have harmed my baby. If I was in the third trimester things could have been different for my unborn child.

I remember watching a documentary on drinking and they used a raw egg to symbolize an embryo and placed it in a glass of whisky, it started frying?

If the mother continues to drink the baby could be addicted to alcohol or the baby could be affected by foetal alcohol syndrome.

The baby's features could be damaged, and it would have all been my fault, I couldn't have lived with that.

Luckily I didn't drink again throughout the rest of my pregnancy.

After a sixteen-hour labour I didn't get the urge to push, so I was placed on the toilet and showed how?

It took me one hour of pushing and my daughter was born weighing 6lb 2ounces and healthy, I was overjoyed.

I was lucky I only had one stitch and no stretch marks. Some poor women had stitches inside and out and could hardly walk.

The moral of this story is "listen to your midwife".

Being alcoholic I opted out of any drugs and on reflection I wonder why?

My husband was away when I could leave the hospital and asked me to stay another night so he could bring us home?

I went home with my mam and dad.

On my first outing with my daughter I was still a bit shaky, so my mam pushed the pram and I walked straight into a lamppost.

Throughout all my pregnancies I smoked.

I switched to low tar cigarettes believing this would make a difference, I later learnt it made no difference whatsoever, I think I was living in cloud cuckoo land.

I hated seeing pregnant women smoke; yet here I was damaging my unborn child and myself.

A year after I had lost my baby Katy I became pregnant with my second daughter. I had contracted shingles and I asked the doctor if it would harm the baby, he said, "Keep your fingers crossed". That really made me feel better; it was a very cruel remark.

I delivered my second daughter, which took nine hours. She weighed in at 7lbs 2 ounces, not being as brave the second time I opted for an epidural.

Unfortunately this only worked down one side of my body. The pain was worse as it was only centred in one side of me.

I was lucky; I didn't have any stitches or any stretch marks.

As you were still able to smoke in the day room off I went dragging half of my numb body, a bit like Lurch in *The Addams Family*.

My daughter was still asleep; I smoked several cigarettes and drank coffee. The day room also gave you the chance to meet other mams and share experiences.

Two years later my son was born weighing 5lb 2ounces, he was a small baby as I had suffered from high blood pressure and oedema, even the soles of my feet were filled with liquid that felt revolting.

I was told to have bed rest, which was a laugh as no one helped me.

Labour lasted over a week, I kept going to the hospital to be returned home as I wasn't dilated enough. On my last visit I was kept in. I was having contractions but the baby wasn't moving down.

The midwife turned me on my side, now that was also painful.

I delivered a beautiful baby boy.

I had chosen to use gas and air; this helped but made me laugh.

Times bringing my children up were a delight.

My marriage failed with my son not yet being one and my daughters three and five years old.

On average, throughout my marriage, I relapsed once a year.

# Chapter Twelve

This has been the hardest chapter to write; I have attempted it many times.

I have had to strike a balance so I can be truthful without hurting my children, even though they are now young adults.

One year into my marriage I was hardly acknowledged mentally or physically.

I was entering in to the phase of being ignored.

Strangely enough he could talk to me over the phone.

This was my fault, I wasn't pretty enough, and I wasn't interesting enough.

I began to feel like a non-entity.

Perhaps as a drunk I didn't deserve to be loved or wanted.

Throughout my ten-year marriage I rarely drank, but I did have relapses.

My ex-husband and his family are heavy drinkers and continued to drink in front of me.

This was my problem not theirs, I was the alcoholic, but I did find this hard.

I hated myself for my relapses and tried so hard to stay sober.

One incident I do remember is that when my parents visited us my husband decided he didn't want to sit at the same table whilst eating. My mam asked why and that if he didn't want them there they could leave.

He was put in his place, 'firmly'.

It was one thing ignoring me, but my parents had always helped us if needed, lending money to us. I found this very rude.

My husband continued to drink heavily, there was always drink in the house, I just had to find it.

When I relapsed I hated myself and the feeling of guilt is hard to overcome and so immense it scared my soul.

I remember one incident when I went to visit a friend, as I got out of the car I remained half in and half out, who knows for how long. I can laugh at this now, I have to otherwise these incidents would bring me crashing down.

I just hope no one saw me in this comprising position.

The things I have done when I drank are overwhelming and if I reflect upon these I could end my life and heaven knows what happened that I don't remember.

If I offended anyone my dad would make sure I apologised to him or her.

This was a humbling experience, with my poor dad trying to explain alcohol addiction.

I am a despicable human being.

I was also lucky if I found my way home.

When my husband and I became estranged I built my life around my marriage. I ran a small children's nursery, I child-minded which enabled me to look after my own children.

My son was not one year old when I divorced my husband who, due to his harrowing ways, plunged me into a nightmare, which lasted several years.

# Chapter Thirteen

I lost so much weight; I was flat chested and didn't feel or look feminine. I lost all of my self-confidence again.

Around this time I suffered with debilitating headaches.

The doctor prescribed a medley of migraine tablets, none of which worked. They were eventually diagnosed as tension headaches.

The doctor then prescribed Amitriptyline and Temazepam. It wasn't long before I was addicted to Temazepam again.

I had run out of these tablets before the repeat prescription was due.

I falsified another prescription, and in due course I was found out, I had to pay for them or return the tablets.

I was terrified so I returned them.

Due to my despicable actions I was struck off the doctor's register.

I had to find another doctor for my children and myself.

I was mortified and so ashamed I could barely live with myself.

This wasn't the real me, this was addiction; it sends you to the bowels of hell.

I had lost the real me a long time ago.

I desperately needed help but I wasn't ready for help, eventually the help would come in the shape of my mam, suffice to say I turned to drink again for help.

This cocktail of drink and medication tablets was choking me.

I functioned normally during the day, I looked after my children, and it was only at night when my demon drink came out to play, I was torturing myself, but I was dying.

It is so hard for people to understand that drink becomes more important than anything you have in life.

A lot of people say, "you chose to drink", which is not necessarily true.

It could be an innocent shandy or a glass of wine, which your parents might give you with a meal.

Drink chose me and wouldn't let go.

You don't choose to be an alcoholic, like no one chooses to be morbidly obese.

It is a disease, some have it, and some don't.

It must be something so deep in your brain you don't realise until it is too late.

Regarding Temazepam; it is only prescribed for a limited period.

On the bottle it states avoid drink, so in my twisted mind it hadn't said don't drink.

It was many years before I realised that this concoction of drink and medication drugs nearly ended my life.

Ignorance is no excuse.

I didn't have any fight left in me. I succumbed to this way of life.

My eldest daughter was told by her father to ring 999 if anything bad happened and rightly so. She was five years old. She was five years old. I was so fearful of not sleeping I began to take my medication earlier and I passed out wherever I was.

I had put my children at risk and didn't deserve to have them.

The ambulance visited me twice and took my children to their father.

I was left in a stupor. My dad commented that no one helped me, perhaps I didn't deserve help, this wasn't a game, it was real life and it involved my beautiful children.

Through drink I had lost my beloved nursery, my friends, my driving licence and, more importantly, nearly my children.

I didn't deserve to live or breathe God's pure air.

Whilst I was struggling to deal with alcoholism and due to the insurmountable problems that drink drops at your door, my brother-in-law said to my dad, "Get her up here".

I moved near my twin sister with four houses in-between us.

# Chapter Fourteen

For as long as I remember I have written and illustrated children's books: The first being about a family of Ladybirds and their antics.

I decided to send them to Ladybird book publishers.

I received a reply stating that their publishing lists were full, and to resubmit them at a later date.

For some strange reason I didn't, I still have this letter today.

Years later I gave them a revamp and submitted them again.

A publishing company called Five Trees Books published them. It was a wonderful experience and we visited Edinburgh to see my books being printed.

Soft toys were made of my Ladybird's complete with their little jackets, not forgetting the spots on their backs, because as we all know, the spots on their backs tell us how old the Ladybirds are.

A head teacher had endorsed these books, they were displayed in bookshops, I spoke on the radio and I read them to the children at their schools. I was in my element.

A lot of the 'nice' people in the office I used to work at most of whom had treated me badly enthused over my books, which I felt had given me a feather in my cap.

Throughout all of my life I have returned again and again to my painting and writing and again to my painting and writing. This has also been my saving grace.

But to write I tended to seclude myself from the outside world and lived inside my head, shutting everything else out.

I was by now carrying my second child. I had felt extremely ill throughout this pregnancy.

A blood test I had from the hospital indicated I may have a slight thyroid problem.

A routine blood test also indicated that my baby might have spina bifida. I was advised to have an amniotic test whereby a needle is inserted in to the spine to test the spinal fluid.

There was a small risk that you might miscarry, which I did one month later.

I had carried my baby for five months.

Whilst I was decorating I started to bleed, I called an ambulance and was admitted to a ward where I was monitored.

My husband didn't come to see me as he was looking after my first daughter. We had many friends who could have looked after her.

As the night progressed I kept getting up to go to the day room for a drink and a smoke.

I kept telling the night nurse I had stomach pains and she kept telling me to go back to bed.

By seven in the morning the pains had gone and I fell asleep.

When the day nurse checked me she said I had lost the baby, I had no help from the night nurse, which had upset me.

I had been alone, I asked if I could see my baby, I was told she was a girl but had been dead for a month, the time I had the amniotic test. I was distraught and called her Katy.

When I was discharged from hospital my dad came to give my daughter and myself a lift to Kendall where my mam was waiting for us.

I had to grieve but things got back to normal, or as normal as possible, but I still felt alone and lost.

# Chapter Fifteen

When I moved to Durham I went selling the surplus books I owned door-to-door.

I did extremely well and the money I earned went straight on special brew.

I remember, to my shame, at one house there was a crate of wine in the porch. I couldn't leave it there so I picked it up and ran, as I ran the wine bottles kept on breaking and I was left with four bottles.

Another shaming incident was when I went to my next-door neighbour and found several bottles of drink on the kitchen table; I scooped them all up and returned home. There hadn't been much alcohol in them and probably they were ready to throw out and I was quite narked at the little alcohol there was.

This incident was ignored and nothing was said to me.

I knew then what burning with shame meant.

I dread to think what they thought of me.

Once in a shop I had secreted special brew cans down my trousers, which were tucked in my boots. The next thing I remember was that the shop seemed to get brighter, an alarm went off and the front and back doors were shut automatically.

Whoever was in the shop with me couldn't get out either; I prayed no one knew me.

I think the manager tried to give me a chance by asking me to put the beer back, but no one was taking my beer away from me. I had made the wrong decision and before you could say "monkey's uncle" I was decked and handcuffed.

I was taken to the police station and put in a cell.

I was ignored for several hours, which I found out was to give me time to sober up.

My fingerprints were taken and I was shaking so much that this took quite a while.

I was eventually released and not charged because it had been my first offence. Perhaps I should have been charged.

This is what the demon drink can do to a person.

I was mortified; it had been an awful experience and should have taught me a lesson.

To be placed in a small cell with a hard bed, a scratchy blanket and a toilet; where anybody could have watched me, no privacy and no way out.

I can't imagine what it would be like to be incarcerated. It was an immense feeling of claustrophobia, absolute terror.

My dad thought that the treatment of being decked and being handcuffed was extreme, but at the end of the day I deserved what I got.

I was a drunk.

How my parents and sister put up with this is also an enigma; I couldn't have done it.

Another incident I remember is that when my parents came to visit me I was drunk. Luckily I saw them first and dashed into my garage and put an old carpet over me and waited until they had gone before I moved.

This was pure madness.

One day when I hadn't been quick enough my mam tried to take a can of special brew off me.

I fought for that can like a mad woman and lost.

My mam was covered in beer.

Of course I had more drink hidden around the house. My mam knew also, finding my hidden drink successfully.

I often forgot where I hid the drink, but as soon as my parents left I bought some more.

If I ran out of money I would send one of my children with a note to my neighbour asking if I could borrow ten pounds, if that failed I sent them to ask my sister, I couldn't go, I stank of drink.

I think my mam developed some sort of radar; she was one step ahead of me, which I resented and it made me hostile.

I withdrew from people; I just wanted to be left alone so I could drink.

Only my mam didn't leave me alone, she was like a bloodhound, always on my trail.

I did find one can she had missed, it was in the oven only I had forgotten this and used the oven, and it became a blue-green sludge.

I used to hide drink in most peculiar places, I will name a few:

Inside my shoes

Under my mattress

In lamp shades

In washing machines

Strapped to my leg

Inside the toilet cistern

Coat pockets, I could go on and on, inside towels, inside bath panels, buried in my garden.

Sometimes I had forgotten where I had hidden them.

I also drank vodka and cream soda, it was delicious.

I went into a curry takeaway, asked for the food to be delivered, I then said I had left the money on the counter; it worked so I tried it again.

It failed and the next day the police were at my door, what I had done was unacceptable and I never did it again.

My sister had noticed the police entering my house, and asked why?

Next to my house there was an infant school and I said they were enquiring about an incident there.

I became adept at lying.

When I was still drinking I dolled myself up and went to the pub down the road from me, leaving my three children asleep, how inexplicable is that?

Perhaps social workers should have been involved, I deserved it.

How I always found my way home I have no idea.

My mam and dad visited me and my dad took me out leaving my mam, she went on the hunt for alcohol and found a small bottle of vodka in my wardrobe, on my return it was on the kitchen worktop.

As my bedroom was being decorated, I blamed it on him.

I don't think my mam believed me.

If there is one thing I have learnt in life due to alcoholism and prescription drugs is that I have wasted chunks of my life, and there must be so much I can't remember, I have come out of that fog into a gentle mist, I can't regain those years: Most of which I wouldn't want to.

I have so many regrets, the worst being my children witnessing my alcoholism at its cruellest.

I did have relationships in Durham and one boyfriend I felt wasn't right for me and I ended the relationship.

For some unexplained reason I had a night's relapse.

I phoned him up and said "I have done something I haven't done for years," he recorded my drunken outpourings and said he had sent a copy to my sister, she didn't listen to this.

He said he would send a copy to social services. This behaviour was so cruel and spiteful, but nevertheless I should have been condemned to Hades.

These relapses are so hard to bear, the guilt, remorse and hatred of myself is inextricable.

For several years I became addicted to Nytol, a sleeping tablet you can buy from a chemist.

I travelled far and wide to purchase these. I used to chew them and achieved a small high and as in any addiction you keep using more and more.

Eventually chemists began to recognise me and stopped serving me, not to be outdone I got a doctor's letter saying I could use these tablets.

Luckily I came out of this madness and stopped using them.

I had no faith in myself. I was on an express train out of control, it was my nemesis, and I was doomed and flawed at such a deep level that I didn't understand myself anymore.

I became hostile, pushing everyone away; I couldn't love myself so how could anyone else?

I was an abomination, a pathetic excuse of a human being. I was lost.

# Chapter Sixteen

I filled every second of every day by painting anything that didn't move, which is not strictly true; my dog Roly sometimes sported blue or silver, or both.

I painted the bath silver. I became quite good at decorating throughout this period.

As my children left for school I painted over any handprints on the doors.

I can't explain that one.

Everything was steam cleaned from the bottom of the house to the top.

I even painted an outside wall white.

I was obsessive in everything I did and would often not go to bed until three in the morning.

At that time I collected porcelain dolls.

I redesigned their clothes and gave them a haircut.

It is only looking back that I can see how ill I was and how broken-hearted and wretched I felt. I was manic.

I would finish my painting regime, shower and get dressed to walk to the nearby shops. I would buy food for tea and my four cans of special brew.

I gave all my children a sandwich box; I used to buy fruit from strawberries to blueberries.

I made little sandwiches with the crusts cut off.

For pudding I had ice cream and banana custard.

My children ate very healthy. They would get excited to see what was in their box.

At the end of the day I used to go to bed the same time as my children.

I took my sleeping tablet and was able to sleep when I wanted, I can still do this today.

Without medication I would be an insomniac waiting for my brain to switch off, but it never did.

I was never able to 'drift off to sleep' or feel that dreamy phase.

The fear, the pure panic and agitation is palpable.

I was living in fairyland and my sleep problem was overlooked due to my serious misuse of alcohol.

These feelings grew like a canker, permeating my whole body and mind.

I had lived a life of pain and angst; it is like I was Jekyll and Hyde.

One part of my brain was screaming at me to stop drinking the other half was screeching to continue to drink.

Until I was ready no one was going to take my drink away, only I could do that.

I then decided to visit charity shops and buy nightwear, from satin pyjamas to satin dressing gowns.

I would shower; do what I needed to do with my special brew by my side.

I then dressed for bed and continued painting; suffice to say I often got paint on my nightwear.

Eventually I started living in long t-shirts; I wore no make up and didn't look in the mirror for nearly seven years.

I stopped cleaning my teeth; I didn't care how I looked.

I also began renting videos and would watch at least four a day.

When my children returned from school, I was in bed and my children did their homework next to me on the bed.

I couldn't help any of them and had no confidence.

# Chapter Seventeen

In Durham I eventually became a recluse, shutting the world out so I couldn't be hurt.

I could walk to the local shops, but if I went anywhere else my sister or dad would take me.

I live like this today.

Health-wise I wasn't too good. I suffered severe dizziness and was referred by doctor for a MRI scan.

The results showed that some platelets were dying in my brain.

Had drinking and smoking caused this, in all honesty I think they did.

The specialist said not to worry too much as I had plenty more.

Alcohol was long gone but I carried on smoking, after all, I had plenty platelets left. It was pure madness, when would I ever learn.

Platelets are the smallest bloody cells. If there was an injury to a bloody vessel, they rapidly clump together to seal the damage.

They stop the bleeding by plugging the broken blood vessel wall and release chemicals that promote clotting.

I also suffer with irritable bowel with complications. This can manifest itself in every undesirable form you can imagine.

Also I have a severe back problem ever since I was pregnant with my son. I had a tens machine and corsets in different sizes.

Part of my lower back doesn't move and also there is inflammation in between the knucklebones.

I am now in treatment with a physiotherapist who uses gentle exercises and bone manipulation; if this doesn't work I may have injections in my spine.

This pain interferes with day-to-day activities and some days cripples me.

Along with this treatment I will have cognitive therapy. I am not sure how this works, but hopefully I can let go of everything negative in my life. One thing I need to lay to rest is the guilt and remorse I feel daily. I acted the way I did due to alcohol misuse, due to a disease.

I am not that person today and haven't been for seventeen years.

Unfortunately I live with one side effect, when I stopped drinking my body-craved sugar. I could eat six doughnuts at once, chocolate and puddings.

I put on three and a half stone, I had always been slim, and this devastated me. I tried so hard and managed to lose the three and a half stone.

I am now ten stone, which is not good but I don't want to lose much weight as I am fifty-eight and I will just be left with loose skin, but I eat a balanced diet and exercise.

# Chapter Eighteen

At one point everything became manageable.

I used to set the table perfectly using different bone china.

I remember one set of china I bought and carried the whole set home which was very heavy. I didn't break any.

Anyone watching would think I was a right idiot, and they would be right.

I then used to make several dinners from lamb to beef; I made four of everything and put them in the fridge.

My children could choose what they wanted.

This didn't sit well with my parents who felt I should cook their dinners fresh every day.

There was a reason that I did this, I was ensuring that my children were at least fed properly before I was incapable.

I have learnt to let some of these feelings go, but some would stay forever.

I let my children down, family and friends.

I hope I have redeemed myself in some way by not drinking.

I will never forgive myself for stealing.

# Chapter Nineteen

I was now entering into the last stage of alcoholism.

I couldn't stop shaking; I shook so violently my mam had to hold my head up for a cup of tea. I couldn't even hold the cup.

I couldn't keep food down and was continuously sick.

I had reached my final 'rock bottom' meaning there is only one way to go and that is up.

Alcoholics who don't reach this stage die.

Alcohol was suffocating the life out of me.

My mam and dad moved from Cumbria to help me, leaving their life and friends behind.

I helped them move in by stealing a bottle of whisky furled in my coat.

I wasn't grateful to them moving, on the contrary, I didn't want anyone around me, and I wanted to be left alone to drink.

I was egotistical but that was part and parcel of being an alcoholic.

I couldn't live like this anymore, it wasn't even an existence.

Most people have suffered a hangover, but what I felt was so much more and the only cure is another drink and at the end this ceased to work.

By now alcohol didn't give me a high; that was long gone.

It is said of drug users that they are chasing the dragon and I believe it is the same for drink.

You try to get that "high" feeling again and again but it is well-nigh impossible.

You just use more and more. The sad thing is you never get that high again and you can kill yourself grasping for it.

You are chasing a puff of air.

I had achieved what I had set out to do, oblivion.

Again and again my family stepped in to help me.

My sister looked after my children on her return from work, and she had three of her own.

I maintain to this day that being alcoholic is hard work, it is all consuming; it is relentless and unforgiving.

I was told my four-year-old son would place his teddies around me. There was gentleness around me that I didn't deserve.

There was kindness around me, but I failed to see it.

My dad took me to Alcoholics Anonymous and he attended a supporting group.

Unfortunately this didn't help me but it has helped countless others.

Mam told me that they had nearly given up on me. I was upstairs in my usual position.

I had bought an alarm clock that kept going off at will.

My parents laughed and my mam, being a bit of a giggler, probably saved my life.

Dad being dad found me a group that helped addicts.

He would deposit me there in the morning and pick me up in the afternoon in time to pick my children up from school.

At this group as I walked in there were drug users, some men who were tattooed and large with teeth missing, there were other alcoholics, too, and self-harmers which I hadn't heard of before.

It was daunting but I met some of the kindest people I know and we all helped each other.

I carried on drinking and began to get nightmares. They were hellish; I remember two - firstly I was covered in sores, and secondly a goat's head appeared out of the wall.

I believe this can happen to drunks, sots and boozers. I didn't like these words but it was who I became.

By the end of that group I was sober and with my head held high, I walked out free and have been sober for seventeen years.

That was another feather in my cap.

Drinking had become a way of life for me.

I also said God gave me two hands; one for a drink and the other for cigarettes.

All I had to do now was relearn life without a drink, and I had a spare hand, which I used for writing and illustrating children's books.

My family has loved me unconditionally and valued my life when I did not.

My mam died over a year ago and I had promised her I would never drink again, and I didn't.

Love your mam when you can, because when she has gone, she's gone.

I had the chance to tell her that I loved her and she saw me sober, which is always what she had strived for.

I haven't always been Miss Doom and Gloom.

I have travelled extensively, embracing different cultures and traditions.

I have experienced joy with my three children.

I need to put this book to bed along with my past. All my children have left home.

I need to move on, and hopefully I can be content with my two dogs, Mia and Charlie, who have enabled me to get out of the house more.

But, I couldn't put this book to bed without telling you a children's story, called *Bertie the Crock*, now could I.

Me, 1961

Aged 14, who had better legs?

I was 16 years old here. I had just started a 2 year art course. I would continue with art throughout my life.

My face would become eventually become bloated along with my body.

Book signing

Book exhibition

# Bertie the Croc
# and Friends

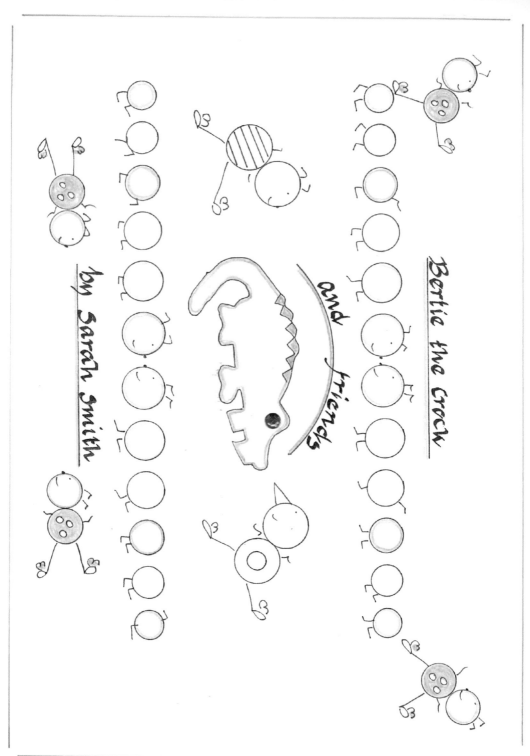

Bertie the Croc

and friends

by Sarah Smith

Bertie the Croc was just swinging by,
He was mean
He was green
And he had lost an eye.

Which gave him a squint
That looked like a wink
If you stared him in the eye.
He looked to his left and saw not a thing as he
only had one eye.

He looked to his right but carried straight on
with just one thought in mind.

He needed two eyes not a squint and a wink,
Or he just could not get by,
Not with just one eye.

You could see the problem Bertie had,
He could only see half of everything,
Not a whole.

He may as well be upside down or live in a hole.

It did not matter you see; he just stayed green
and mean.

That is, until he could find his missing eye.

He went back to the river with a green splash.

He could get along faster and cut quite a dash.

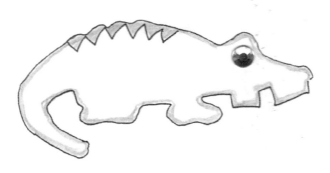

Without any warning he had a great shock.

A bumble bee landed on his knee.

"What do you want?" Bertie said, "Are you trying to frighten me? Is that a sting pointing straight at me?"

"Oh no, I am just a humble bumble bee."

He laughed at the croc and said "How can you be green and mean, with a squint in your eye that looks like a wink, if I stare you in the eye? Can you only see half of me?"

With a tear in his eye he looked to the sky
Hoping the bumble bee would not see.

But he did and he said "Come with me, I'll find
your eye for you. Put these cool shades on and
no one will see that you just have one eye. It will
be between me and you."

With a spring in his step and a song in his heart
he followed the humble bumble bee.

Over woodland and bracken the two friends went, and guess what?
When they turned around there were others to see.

As the story goes by a Chinese whisper, everyone knew that the big green crock had lost one eye and had a squint that looked like a wink when you stared at him in one eye.

What was it like for the big green crock to have only one eye?

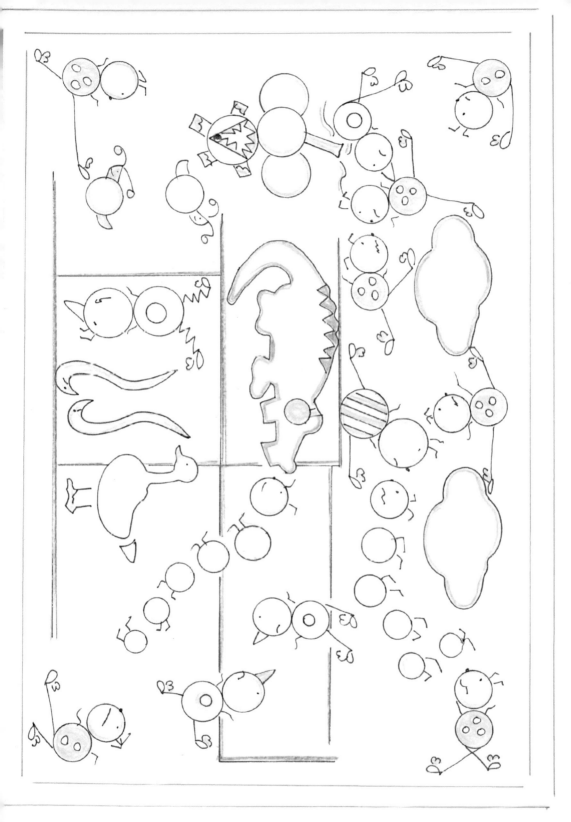

No one knew, so what did they do?

They all shut one eye, which was a mistake as they all fell down, just like so.

The big green croc looked at his friends in glee.

"Now you'll look as silly as me."

With friends in tow off they went in search of you know what.

An eye for the big green croc that had a squint
In his eye that looked like a wink,
If you stared him in the eye.

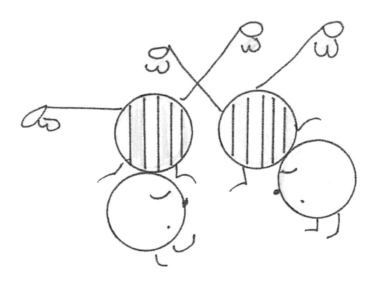

The night was upon them
Before you could say
"It's dark and it's starry and we have had a bad
day."

They looked at each other by the pale moon light
but Bertie the Croc was nowhere in sight.

"Oh goodness me," said the humble bumble bee.
He had his cool shades on, they won't do,
He won't be able to see, don't you agree.

They called the croc but nothing was heard.

They sat on a log to think and to think because
five heads are better than one, don't you think.

Before they all knew they were on the ground
and the big green crock had been found.

"I was on the log you were sitting on." That will
teach you a lesson or two. To look where you sit
or you may get a nip, and that just would not do.

They camped by the fire until daylight returned.

All friends together in this big wide world.

When they awoke they were sad to see Bertie's shades were up a tree.

They looked at each other not once but twice as there was also a snake up in the tree.

He slithered part way down as cool as he could be.

But he was wearing Bertie's shades and could not see.

The shades rolled away and all the friends could see Bertie's eye was up there in the tree.

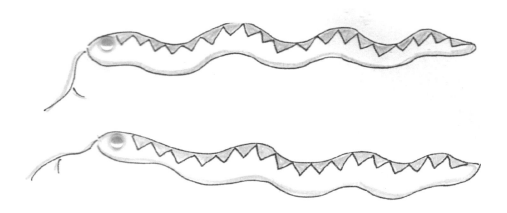

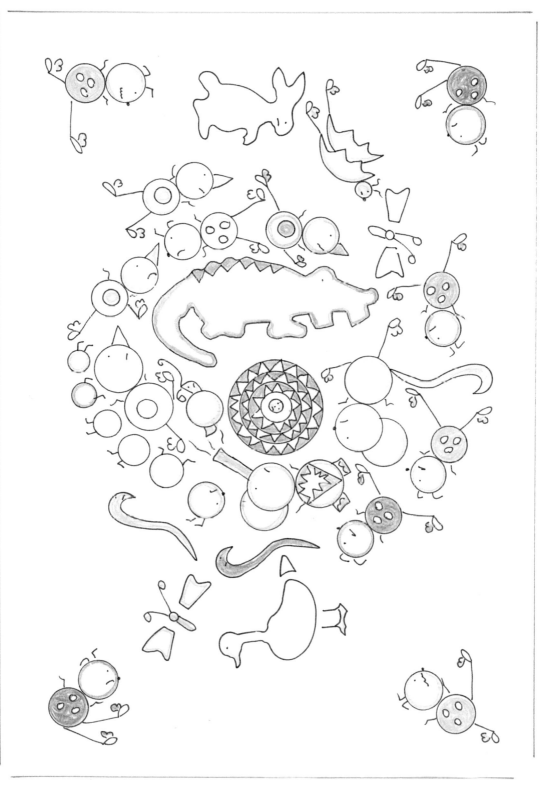

They looked at the snake and he looked back, for he only had one eye you see.

Bertie had his eye back but they were all in shock because oh dear the snake had not.

The snake curled up as tight as he could be and said "Why are you staring at me, his eye didn't fit me."

So we had one green croc with both his eyes, but the problem remained the snake had not.

The snake was hissing and he was in no mood for kissing
Until he could find his eye.

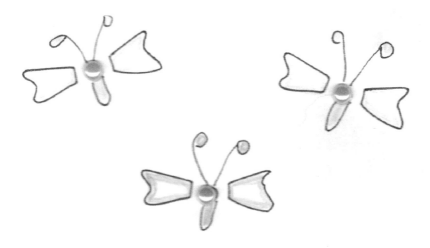

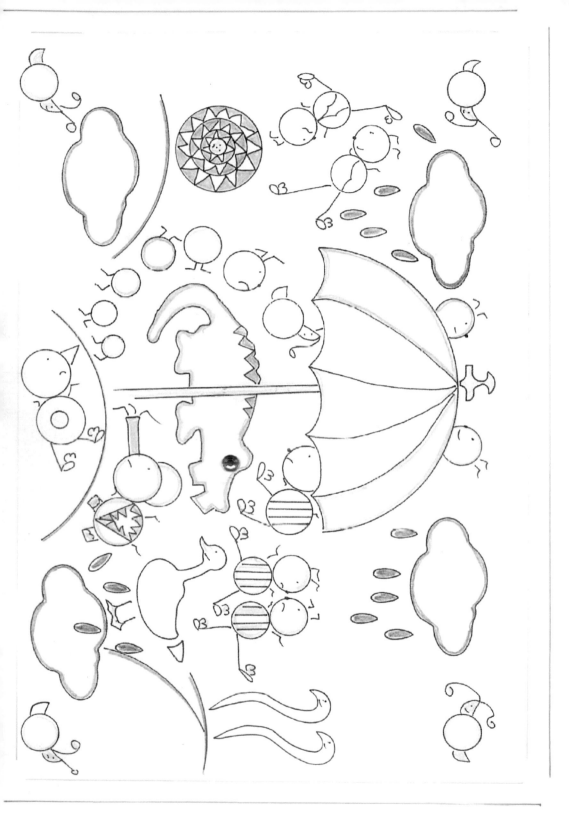

Where do they go from here? No one was sure but all agreed to meet back at six, and off they went to do their bit.

The wind got up, the rain fell down and everybody went round and round.

All ending up in a soggy wet pile.

They found an umbrella next to a stile and huddled together a while.

The sun came up, the umbrella went down and off they went towards the town.

There was a fish in the pond that looked quite bright, perhaps he knew?

A talking fish that was quite a delight, they hoped he would put them right,

"I'm only a fish, what would I know? But I'm a fish with a wish."

"Is that a cat looking at me?"

It was a very posh cat they all agreed

A cat with three eyes, how could that be?

Look carefully, can't you see it is shining on her collar.

Is that a diamante?

They looked again and all agreed that was no diamante
And the snake with a shake found his eye.

The fish with a wish jumped back in his pond, with his wish intact, that was a fact.

"Don't bring that cat near me."

"Not a chance," said the snake with both his eyes and a shake.

"It's not a friend of mine."

So, we had a fish with a wish, a big green croc that had lost his mean, even though he was big and green.

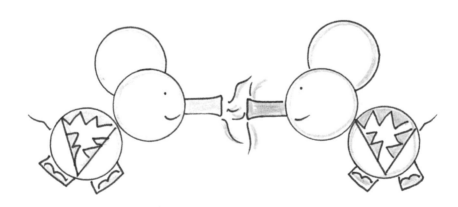

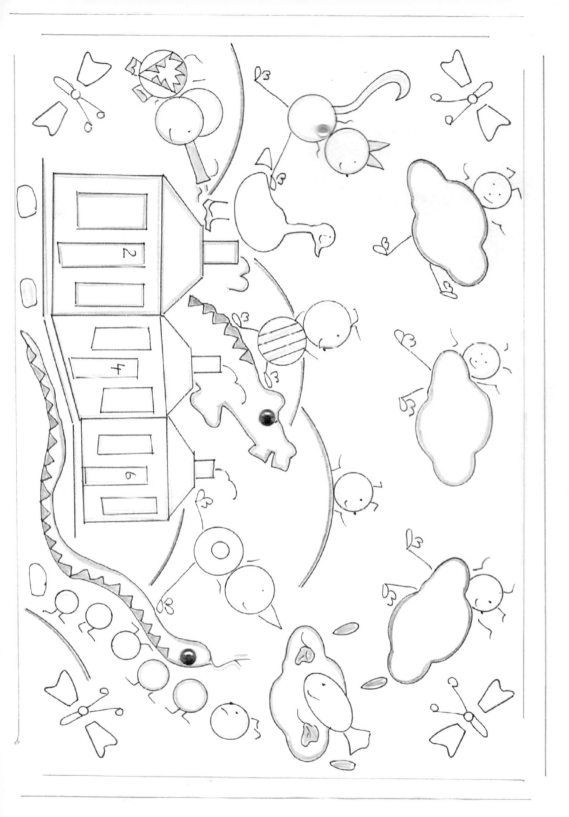

We had a cat with a frown, a snake with two eyes and a shake.

They had all made friends and were as happy as could be.

They walked back together in this big wide world.

Except... the caterpillar was nowhere to be seen.

Perhaps he had climbed a tree.

"Oh look," said the croc "it is plain to see that the caterpillar is not in a tree."

He is over there where he should be, as a
beautiful butterfly for the world to see.

But... that is another story, don't you agree.